WHISPERS IN THE MIST

ELENA RETURNS TO HER MIST-SHROUDED HOMETOWN AND, ALONGSIDE OLD FRIENDS, UNCOVERS A DARK SECRET

BY HANNAH JONES

Contents

Chapter 1. The Town of Hollow's End 5

Chapter 2. Shadows in the Mist 12

Chapter 3. Into the Mist 20

Chapter 4. The Lurking Threat 29

Chapter 5. Shadows in the Night 38

Chapter 6. The Secrets of Hollow's End 46

Chapter 7. The Cloaked Threat 55

Chapter 8. Shadows of the Past 64

Chapter 9. Descent into Darkness 73

Chapter 10. The Heart of Hollow's End 82

*Copyright © 2024 Elena Sinclair
All Rights Reserved.*

Chapter 1. The Town of Hollow's End

Elena Rivers felt a chill run down her spine as she drove into Hollow's End. The thick, swirling fog cloaked the small town, making it seem like it was teetering on the edge of a forgotten world. Her hands tightened around the steering wheel, and her mind raced with excitement and apprehension.

This was it. The place where people vanished without a trace. The place where Evelyn Grayson disappeared five years ago.

Elena had been chasing this story for months. Every lead, every source, had led her here. Hollow's End, a town that barely appeared on maps and where the locals kept to themselves. She parked her car in front of the only inn in town—*The Silver Lantern*—and stepped out, the mist curling around her legs like ghostly fingers.

As she entered the dimly lit inn, a bell chimed, and a middle-aged woman behind the counter looked up from her book. Her eyes narrowed slightly.

"Welcome to *The Silver Lantern*. You must be Elena Rivers," the woman said, her voice betraying no emotion.

Elena blinked. She hadn't introduced herself yet.

"Word travels fast in Hollow's End," the woman added with a small smile. "I'm Rose, the innkeeper."

Elena nodded, trying to ignore the unease bubbling in her stomach. "I suppose it does. I called ahead. I'll be staying for a while."

Rose handed her a key. "Room 3, upstairs. Breakfast is served at seven. Hollow's End isn't much for nightlife, so don't expect anything too exciting. Except…" Rose hesitated, glancing toward the window where the fog pressed against the glass like a living thing. "Except the mist."

"The mist?" Elena asked, her curiosity piqued.

Rose's smile faltered. "You'll see."

Elena wanted to ask more, but the innkeeper turned away, effectively ending the conversation. Shrugging off the odd exchange, Elena grabbed her bag and headed upstairs. The inn was old, with creaky floors and dark wood paneling that seemed to absorb all light.

Her room was small but cozy, with a single window overlooking the town's main street. As she unpacked her things, her mind wandered to her real reason for being here.

Evelyn Grayson's disappearance.

Five years ago, the young woman had vanished without a trace. Her brother, Luke, had searched tirelessly, but the case went cold. No leads, no body, no answers. Elena had stumbled upon the story while researching another case, and something about it had gripped her. Evelyn wasn't the only one. Over the past two decades, at least six people had gone missing in Hollow's End, all under strange circumstances.

She pulled out her laptop and opened the file she had been working on. Names, dates, places—it was all there. She read through the list again, noting the eerie similarities between the disappearances. The victims had all been last seen near the town's outskirts, where the mist seemed thickest. Locals whispered about strange lights in the fog, about voices calling from the darkness.

But no one talked openly.

Elena had tried reaching out to the police chief in Hollow's End before coming, but he'd refused to speak with her. No one here wanted to discuss what was happening. It was as if the town itself was guarding its secrets.

A knock on her door startled her out of her thoughts. She opened it to find a tall, dark-haired man standing in the hallway, his expression hard to read. His eyes were the first thing she noticed—dark, intense, and haunted.

"Luke Grayson," he said, his voice low. "You're the reporter."

Elena felt a jolt of recognition. She had seen his picture while researching the case. He had been a detective in the city before returning to his hometown after his sister's disappearance.

"Yeah," she replied. "Elena Rivers. I'm investigating the disappearances here."

Luke leaned against the doorframe, arms crossed. "You should leave."

Elena raised an eyebrow. "That's a bit harsh, considering I just got here."

"This town isn't safe," he said, his tone grave. "People vanish. You could be next."

Elena's heart raced, but she didn't back down. "I'm here to find out what happened to your sister, Luke. Don't you want answers?"

Something flickered in his eyes, a mix of pain and anger. "Of course I do," he muttered, his jaw tight. "But there are forces at work here you can't understand. You're playing with fire."

Elena stepped closer, her voice softening. "Help me, then. You know this town better than anyone. Together, we might be able to figure out what's going on."

For a moment, Luke didn't say anything. He just stared at her, as if weighing his options. Then, with a sigh, he pushed away from the doorframe.

"I'm meeting a contact tomorrow," he said. "Someone who might know something. Be ready at dawn. But remember this, Elena—once you go down this road, there's no turning back."

Elena nodded, her pulse quickening. "I'm not going anywhere."

Luke gave her one last look before turning and walking away, disappearing into the shadows of the old inn. Elena closed the door, her mind racing.

The fog outside thickened, and the whispers in the mist seemed to grow louder. She wasn't sure if it was her imagination, but she thought she heard someone calling her name.

The mystery of Hollow's End had begun.

Chapter 2. Shadows in the Mist

Elena's sleep was restless. The whispering outside her window seemed to ebb and flow with the mist, like something alive, trying to get in. Every time she closed her eyes, she saw Evelyn Grayson's face—blurry, distorted, calling for help but vanishing just before Elena could reach her.

When her phone buzzed at the crack of dawn, she jolted awake, heart pounding. A single text from Luke: *Meet me at the old church. Don't be late.*

She groaned, rubbing the sleep from her eyes and glancing out the window. The fog was still there, thicker now, swirling ominously over the street. Whatever had been pulling her to Hollow's End was stronger this morning, a strange magnetic pull she couldn't explain. As she threw on her jacket and laced up her boots, she couldn't shake the feeling that something was watching her.

Outside, the town was eerily quiet. Even the birds didn't chirp. The fog swallowed every sound, muffling her footsteps as she made her way toward the old church Luke had mentioned. It was perched on a hill at the town's edge, its bell tower rising out of the mist like a ghostly sentinel.

The church was abandoned—had been for years, according to her research. Some of the locals believed it was haunted, and most stayed away. As Elena approached, she could see why. The building's windows were shattered, the doors warped from years of disuse, and the overgrown graveyard surrounding it gave the place an even more unsettling vibe.

Luke was already there, leaning against the church's rusted gates, his eyes scanning the mist for any movement. He wore a heavy jacket, the collar pulled up to shield against the cold. When he saw her approach, he straightened, his face unreadable.

"You made it," he said simply.

"I said I wasn't going anywhere," Elena replied, standing next to him. "What's this contact of yours going to tell us?"

Luke didn't answer right away. Instead, he turned and led her through the gates, the iron creaking as it swung open. The gravestones around them loomed out of the fog like forgotten memories, each one marking a life swallowed by the secrets of Hollow's End.

"My contact is a former police officer," Luke finally said as they walked toward the back of the church. "He was on the force when Evelyn disappeared. There were things… covered up. Things that don't add up. He started asking questions, and suddenly, he was forced into early retirement."

"Sounds like a conspiracy," Elena said, her pulse quickening.

"It is," Luke replied darkly. "And if we're not careful, we'll be the next ones they bury."

They rounded the back of the church, where an old shed stood hidden in the mist. The door creaked open, revealing a grizzled man in his fifties with a weathered face and a cigarette dangling from his lips. His eyes darted nervously, and he gave a curt nod when he saw Luke.

"This her?" the man asked, his voice raspy.

Luke nodded. "Elena Rivers, the journalist."

The man grunted. "Hope you know what you're getting into, lady. This town chews people up and spits them out."

"I'm willing to take the risk," Elena said, holding her ground.

The man smirked, but it was a grim expression. "Suit yourself."

He motioned for them to step inside the shed. It was cramped, with tools scattered haphazardly on shelves, and a single dim lightbulb swayed overhead. Elena felt claustrophobic almost immediately, but she tried to focus on the task at hand.

"Name's Garrett," the man said, lighting another cigarette. "I worked for the Hollow's End Police Department for twenty years. Everything was fine until folks started disappearing. At first, we thought they were runaways or just unlucky travelers, but after the third one vanished without a trace, we knew something else was going on."

He exhaled a plume of smoke, his eyes narrowing. "Then came the whispers."

Elena's heart skipped a beat. "The whispers?"

Garrett nodded. "The mist. It's not natural. Everyone in town knows it. At night, you can hear things in it—voices, calling out. People say they hear their loved ones, or people who've gone missing. My partner heard his mother's voice one night… she'd been dead for ten years."

Luke shifted uncomfortably. "You're saying the mist is connected to the disappearances?"

"I'm saying the mist is *alive*," Garrett said bluntly. "And whatever's hiding in it, it wants more people."

Elena felt a cold shiver run down her spine. This was sounding more like a horror story than a mystery, but she had to remind herself that there had to be a rational explanation. Maybe the town's isolation had made people superstitious. Or maybe there was a predator lurking in the fog, using psychological tricks to lure people out.

"Did you hear anything the night Evelyn disappeared?" she asked, glancing at Luke.

Luke's jaw tightened. "No. I was out of town that night, on a case. By the time I got back, she was already gone. No trace, no signs of struggle. Just… gone."

Garrett leaned forward, his voice lowering to a conspiratorial whisper. "That's because they don't struggle. The mist calls to them. It gets inside their heads. Makes them believe something's out there waiting for them."

"Who's 'they'?" Elena asked, her curiosity piqued.

Garrett looked over his shoulder, as if expecting someone to be listening. "The Order of the Crimson Veil."

Luke stiffened beside her, and Elena could feel the tension rolling off him. She had never heard of this group before, but it clearly struck a nerve with Luke.

"What is the Order of the Crimson Veil?" she pressed.

Garrett stubbed out his cigarette, his hands trembling slightly. "A cult. They've been around for as long as this town has. They worship the mist. They believe it's some kind of ancient force that needs to be fed. Every few years, they take someone—sacrifice them to whatever's out there. And the town lets them."

Elena stared at him in disbelief. "That's insane."

"Is it?" Garrett shot back. "Look around. Why else would people vanish without a trace? Why else would no one talk? Everyone here knows. They just pretend they don't."

A heavy silence fell over the room. Elena's mind raced, trying to process everything Garrett had just told her. Was it possible? Could a secret cult be behind the disappearances?

Before she could ask another question, there was a sudden thump outside the shed.

All three of them froze. Garrett's eyes widened in fear, and Luke instinctively moved in front of Elena.

The whispers outside grew louder, swirling in the mist.

"Elena," Luke whispered, his voice tight. "We need to get out of here."

But it was too late.

The door creaked open, and the mist began to pour in.

Chapter 3. Into the Mist

The fog slithered into the shed like a living thing, its thick, silvery tendrils curling around their feet and climbing toward their knees. Elena's breath caught in her throat, her pulse hammering in her ears. She had never seen fog move like this. It wasn't just the mist that was unnatural—it was the silence that came with it. The world outside had gone completely still.

Garrett scrambled to the corner, fumbling with a rusted old shotgun hanging on the wall. His hands shook, but he managed to grab it and cock it, the sound loud and jarring in the silence. "We need to leave. Now."

Luke didn't need convincing. He grabbed Elena's wrist, his grip firm but urgent. "Stay close. Don't listen to anything."

"Listen to what?" Elena asked, her voice barely a whisper, fear creeping into her chest.

"The voices," Luke said darkly, his eyes scanning the thickening mist outside. "Just keep your focus. We're getting out of here."

Garrett pushed past them, kicking open the shed door. The swirling fog outside seemed almost to recoil for a moment, only to press back in, surrounding them from every angle. The whispers came next—soft at first, like a breeze brushing against Elena's ears. She strained to hear the words, but they were too faint. Too distant.

Then, as they stepped out into the open, the voices became clearer.

"Elena…"

Her heart froze. It was her mother's voice—gentle, familiar, calling her name in the way she had when Elena was a child. But that was impossible. Her mother had died five years ago. She shook her head, trying to shake the sound away. But it grew louder.

"Elena… come to me…"

The mist thickened around them, tendrils of it brushing against her cheeks like cold fingers. She knew it wasn't real. It couldn't be. And yet, every instinct in her body screamed for her to turn and follow the voice. It was pulling her, tugging at her memories, at her grief.

Luke's hand tightened around her wrist, grounding her. "Don't listen," he whispered, his voice cutting through the fog. "It's not real. It's the mist. Just keep moving."

Garrett led them through the graveyard, his shotgun held up as if ready to fire at any moment, though Elena doubted a gun could stop whatever was out there. The gravestones rose up out of the mist like jagged teeth, and the voices continued to swirl around them, each one more desperate than the last.

"Elena, I need you…"

"I'm waiting for you…"

The voices tugged at her, but Luke's presence kept her steady. She didn't let go of his hand, no matter how much her mind tried to convince her to turn around and follow the sound of her mother's voice.

Garrett stopped abruptly, raising his hand in a signal to be quiet. Ahead, the fog had thickened to the point where they could barely see five feet in front of them. But there was something else—faint, shadowy figures moving in the mist. They were too far to make out clearly, but they were coming closer.

"Get down," Luke hissed, pulling Elena behind a large gravestone. Garrett crouched next to them, his hands trembling around the shotgun.

Elena's heart pounded in her chest as she peered through the fog, trying to make out the shapes. They moved slowly, almost deliberately, as if searching for something—or someone.

"What are they?" she whispered, her breath clouding in the cold air.

"The Order," Luke said, his voice grim. "The ones Garrett told you about."

Elena's throat tightened. "What do they want?"

"They're looking for their next offering," Garrett muttered under his breath. "Someone to give to the mist."

Elena's skin crawled. The idea of a secret cult hunting people down in the fog, offering them up to some unknown force, was terrifying enough. But the fact that it might be real—*that* sent her heart racing.

The shadows moved closer, their footsteps nearly silent in the mist. They seemed to glide over the ground, their movements inhumanly smooth. Elena tried to make out faces, but the fog obscured everything except their outlines.

Luke leaned in close, his breath warm against her ear. "On my signal, we're going to make a run for it. Stay low. Don't look back."

Elena nodded, her pulse thrumming. She was scared, but she trusted him.

Garrett's eyes were wide, his face pale, but he nodded too. "I'll cover you."

The whispers grew louder, swirling around them like a chorus of ghostly voices, each one more insistent than the last. Elena's grip on Luke's hand tightened. Her mother's voice echoed in her head, growing more desperate. *"Come to me, Elena. Don't leave me..."*

She shook her head, fighting the pull, but it was growing stronger. Her vision blurred as tears filled her eyes. The mist seemed to wrap around her mind, tugging at her memories, at her grief, at the part of her that had never fully healed from her mother's death.

Luke must have sensed her struggle because he squeezed her hand harder. "Stay with me," he whispered fiercely. "Focus on me. We're getting out of this."

Elena blinked back the tears, nodding. She couldn't afford to lose herself now. Not when they were so close to danger.

Luke glanced toward the figures, then back at her. "Now."

Without hesitation, he pulled her up, and they sprinted through the graveyard, ducking low as they weaved between gravestones. Garrett stayed behind them, his shotgun ready, but he didn't fire. The figures in the mist hadn't seen them yet—or if they had, they hadn't reacted.

Elena's heart pounded in her chest as they ran. The fog clung to them, trying to slow them down, but Luke was relentless, guiding her through the maze of gravestones with the precision of someone who had done this before.

Suddenly, a low, guttural sound echoed through the mist—like a growl, deep and primal. It sent a shiver down Elena's spine. Whatever that sound was, it wasn't human.

Garrett froze, his eyes wide with fear. "That's them. The ones who—"

A figure emerged from the mist right in front of them, tall and shrouded in darkness. It moved toward them with deliberate slowness, its face hidden beneath a hood, but Elena could feel its eyes on her.

Luke pushed her behind him, his hand going to the gun holstered at his side. "Get back."

The figure stopped, tilting its head as if studying them. For a moment, no one moved. The whispers in the mist grew louder, more frantic.

And then, the figure spoke.

"Elena Rivers," it said, its voice unnervingly calm. "You don't belong here."

Elena's blood ran cold. She had never seen this person before, but they knew her name. They knew *who she was*.

Luke stepped forward, his jaw tight. "Stay away from her."

The figure didn't move, but the shadows around them seemed to shift, like the mist itself was alive, swirling in response to the figure's presence.

"You should have left when you had the chance," the figure said softly, almost regretfully. "Now the mist will take you both."

Without warning, it lunged toward them, the fog erupting into chaos.

Chapter 4. The Lurking Threat

Luke's reaction was instantaneous. He pushed Elena out of the figure's path, drawing his gun in a fluid motion. Garrett raised his shotgun, his finger hovering over the trigger, but the figure moved impossibly fast, disappearing into the mist before they could react.

Elena stumbled, catching herself on a gravestone, her breath ragged as she tried to make sense of what had just happened. The air felt colder, heavier, like the mist was closing in on them, tightening its grip.

"Elena!" Luke called, his voice sharp. "Are you okay?"

"I'm fine," she gasped, steadying herself, though her heart raced wildly. "What the hell was that?"

Luke's face was grim as he scanned the swirling fog, his gun still drawn. "One of them."

"One of *what*?"

"The Order's hunters," Garrett muttered, his voice trembling as he checked his surroundings, shotgun raised. "They're the ones who go out into the mist to find people. Once they've marked you, they don't stop."

Elena's chest tightened. "What do you mean, 'marked'?"

Luke grabbed her arm, pulling her toward a narrow pathway that led out of the graveyard. "We don't have time to explain. We need to move, now."

The fog seemed to pulse with a malevolent energy as they ran, shadows darting in and out of sight, always just out of reach. The whispers grew louder, more insistent, tugging at Elena's mind like invisible hands. She could still hear her mother's voice calling to her, but now, it was mixed with others—voices she didn't recognize, all pleading, begging, urging her to come closer.

"Elena... don't leave me..."

"I'm here... I'm waiting..."

She squeezed her eyes shut, willing herself to block out the sound, but it only grew louder, more suffocating. The mist wasn't just a natural phenomenon; it was alive, feeding on her fear, on her memories.

Luke's grip on her arm was the only thing keeping her anchored in reality. His presence was solid, real, a lifeline in the storm of madness swirling around her.

She clung to him, her steps faltering as the ground beneath them became uneven, the old cobblestones slick with dew.

"Keep moving," Luke urged, his voice low but firm. "We're almost out."

They reached the edge of the graveyard, where a broken-down fence marked the boundary between the church grounds and the dense forest beyond. Luke vaulted over it, pulling Elena with him, while Garrett scrambled after them, his breath labored.

The mist didn't seem to follow them into the woods. It lingered at the edge of the graveyard, swirling like an angry cloud, but it didn't cross the threshold. The whispers faded, leaving only the eerie stillness of the forest behind.

Elena leaned against a tree, trying to catch her breath. Her entire body trembled from the adrenaline, and her mind struggled to process what had just happened.

"I didn't think it was real," she whispered, staring into the darkness where the mist still writhed. "The stories, the whispers... all of it. I thought it was just superstition."

Luke holstered his gun, his face set in a hard line. "It's real, Elena. The Order controls the mist. They've been doing it for centuries. That's how they keep the town in their grip."

"But what *is* it?" Elena asked, her voice shaky. "The mist, the voices... how is that possible?"

Garrett sat on a nearby rock, wiping sweat from his brow, his shotgun resting across his lap. He looked exhausted, defeated. "The Order worships something old. Something that's been here long before any of us. They believe the mist is its way of communicating—of feeding."

Elena shivered. "Feeding on what?"

"On us," Garrett said grimly. "Our fear, our memories, our souls. The people who disappear... they're not just gone. They're *taken*."

The words sent a chill down Elena's spine. She had come to Hollow's End expecting to uncover some kind of conspiracy, but this was far beyond anything she could have imagined. The mist, the cult, the disappearances—it was all connected, and it was more terrifying than she'd ever dreamed.

Luke's expression softened as he looked at her, his hand brushing lightly against her arm. "I tried to warn you. This isn't just a story, Elena. It's dangerous. And now, they know you're here."

She swallowed hard, the weight of his words sinking in. She had always been drawn to danger, to uncovering the truth, but this… this was something else entirely. She wasn't just investigating a mystery anymore. She was part of it.

"We need to get out of here," Luke continued, glancing at Garrett. "The longer we stay in the open, the more vulnerable we are."

"Where can we go?" Elena asked, her voice tinged with panic. "The Order controls the town. If they know we're here, how are we supposed to stay safe?"

"There's a cabin," Luke said, his voice steady. "Deep in the woods. It belonged to my father. No one knows about it. We'll be safe there for the night."

Elena nodded, trusting him despite the fear gnawing at her insides. Luke had been through this before—he had lost his sister to the mist, and he wasn't about to let it take anyone else.

Garrett stood, slinging the shotgun over his shoulder. "I hope you're right, Grayson. Because if they find us out here…"

"They won't," Luke interrupted, his tone firm. "Not if we move now."

Without another word, they set off into the woods, the trees towering above them like silent sentinels. The air was damp, and the forest floor was soft with moss, making their footsteps nearly silent. The further they went, the quieter the world became, as if the very forest was holding its breath, waiting.

Elena stayed close to Luke, her heart still racing from their encounter in the graveyard. The darkness of the woods felt different from the mist—not as menacing, but still oppressive, as if the shadows themselves were watching.

They walked for what felt like hours, the path winding deeper and deeper into the forest. Elena's legs ached, and her mind raced with questions. How had

Luke lived with this for so long? How had the town let this happen?

Eventually, they reached a small clearing, where a weathered cabin stood nestled among the trees. It was old, with moss growing up the sides and the windows dark, but it looked sturdy enough. Luke approached it first, pulling a key from his pocket and unlocking the door.

"We'll be safe here," he said, stepping inside and motioning for Elena and Garrett to follow. "At least for tonight."

Elena stepped inside, the warmth of the cabin a welcome contrast to the cold outside. The interior was sparse but functional—a few chairs, a small table, and a fireplace that Luke immediately began to stoke. The walls were lined with shelves filled with old books and hunting equipment, a reminder of the man Luke's father must have been.

As the fire crackled to life, Elena sat down, her mind spinning. She wanted to ask Luke more about the Order, about what they were up against, but she was exhausted. The day's events had left her mentally and physically drained.

Luke sat across from her, his eyes fixed on the fire. "Get some rest," he said quietly. "We'll figure out our next move in the morning."

Elena nodded, though she wasn't sure how she would be able to sleep with everything that had happened. But as the warmth of the fire seeped into her bones, her eyelids grew heavy, and she let herself drift off, the whispers of the mist still echoing faintly in the back of her mind.

Chapter 5. Shadows in the Night

Elena awoke with a start, her heart pounding in her chest. The cabin was quiet, the fire having burned down to embers. For a moment, she thought everything had been a dream—the mist, the voices, the Order—but the cold fear that settled over her said otherwise.

She glanced around, her eyes adjusting to the dim light. Garrett was slumped in a chair near the door, his shotgun propped against the wall, snoring softly. Luke, however, was nowhere to be seen.

Panic flared in her chest. Where had he gone? She stood up, her legs stiff from exhaustion, and crossed the small room to the door. The night outside was pitch black, the forest thick with shadows.

"Elena..."

The whisper was faint but unmistakable. She froze, her breath catching in her throat. It wasn't her mother's voice this time. It was Luke's.

"Elena, I need you..."

Her pulse quickened. Luke was out there, in the darkness, calling to her. She didn't understand how—

she hadn't heard him leave—but the sound of his voice was unmistakable. It was soft, pleading, just outside the cabin, as though he needed help.

She reached for the door handle, her hand trembling. Something deep inside her warned against it, told her not to go out there, but the pull was strong. What if Luke was in trouble? What if the mist had him?

"Elena, please…"

Her fingers brushed the cold metal of the door handle when a firm hand grabbed her arm, yanking her back.

"What are you doing?" Luke's voice was low and tense, and when she turned, she saw him standing right behind her, his face etched with concern.

"I… I heard you," Elena stammered, pulling her hand back from the door. "I heard you outside, calling my name."

"That wasn't me," Luke said, his voice dark. "That was the mist."

Elena's blood ran cold as the realization sank in. The mist had imitated Luke's voice—just as it had used her mother's—to lure her out. She could have stepped outside into the darkness, into whatever waited in the fog, if Luke hadn't stopped her.

Her knees felt weak, and she sank onto the nearest chair, her hands trembling. "How is it doing this? How is it... mimicking people?"

Luke knelt in front of her, his eyes filled with a mixture of anger and something else—fear. "It doesn't just mimic. It knows what you're afraid of. It feeds off your memories, your grief. It knows what will break you, and it uses that against you."

Elena stared at him, her mind reeling. "So, it's... alive?"

"In a way," Luke said quietly. "The Order calls it 'the Shadow'—an ancient force that's tied to the mist. It doesn't just take people, Elena. It consumes them. Their memories, their souls. It uses the voices of the dead to draw you in, and once you're lost in the mist, you're gone. Forever."

She shuddered, her stomach churning. The idea that something so ancient, so malevolent, could have such power was horrifying. It was no longer just a mystery to solve; it was a fight for survival.

Garrett stirred from his chair, blinking groggily. "What's going on?" he muttered, rubbing his eyes.

"Nothing," Luke said quickly, standing up. "Just a close call."

Garrett grunted, glancing at Elena with mild concern before settling back into his seat. "Figures. This place is a nightmare. Can't believe I let you talk me into coming back here, Grayson."

Luke didn't respond, his gaze fixed on Elena. "You need to be careful," he said softly. "It will try again. And next time, it might be harder to resist."

Elena nodded, her throat dry. She had nearly fallen for it—nearly opened the door to whatever was lurking outside. She didn't want to think about what might have happened if Luke hadn't been there.

The night passed slowly, with an oppressive tension that made it impossible for Elena to sleep again. The forest outside was eerily quiet, and every creak of the cabin made her heart jump. Luke kept watch by the window, his expression unreadable as he stared into the darkness.

It wasn't until the first light of dawn began to filter through the trees that the heavy silence seemed to lift. The mist had retreated with the coming of morning, and though the shadows still lingered between the trees, they no longer felt as suffocating.

"We need to leave," Luke said, breaking the silence. "It's not safe here anymore. The Order knows we're close. They'll come for us."

Garrett nodded, standing up and stretching. "What's the plan, then? We can't just keep running."

Luke hesitated, his jaw clenched as if weighing his options. "There's one place we haven't searched yet. The old library in town. It's where my sister was last seen before she disappeared."

Elena frowned. "The library? How would that help?"

"There are records there," Luke explained. "Old ones. My father used to go there to research the Order and the mist. If we can find what he was looking for, maybe we can understand how to stop it."

Garrett scoffed. "You really think we can stop this thing? Your old man spent years trying, and look where it got him."

Luke's eyes darkened. "We don't have a choice."

Elena looked between the two men, her heart heavy with uncertainty. She wanted to believe they could find answers, that there was a way to end the terror that gripped Hollow's End, but part of her feared they were already too late. The Order had been in control for centuries. How could they possibly hope to defeat something so powerful?

Still, she couldn't shake the feeling that the library held something important. The fact that Luke's sister had disappeared from there couldn't be a coincidence. There had to be something—some clue that would lead them to the truth.

"Let's go," she said, her voice steadier than she felt. "We can't stay here. We need to find those records."

Luke nodded, his gaze softening as he looked at her. "We'll figure this out, Elena. We'll stop them."

She wanted to believe him. But as they gathered their things and prepared to leave the cabin, she couldn't shake the feeling that something was watching them, lurking just beyond the trees.

The library might hold the answers they were looking for, but the mist wasn't done with them yet. And as they stepped out into the cold morning air, Elena knew that whatever waited for them in Hollow's End would be far more dangerous than anything they had faced so far.

The shadows in the night were just the beginning.

Chapter 6. The Secrets of Hollow's End

The town of Hollow's End was unnervingly quiet as Luke, Elena, and Garrett approached the old library. The early morning light filtered through the narrow streets, casting long shadows that made everything feel sharper, more menacing. Elena kept her eyes on the crumbling buildings, their windows dark and hollow, as if the town itself had been drained of life. The oppressive silence only deepened the tension swirling in her chest.

"Stay alert," Luke whispered, his gaze flicking to the rooftops and alleyways. "The Order has eyes everywhere."

Elena tightened her grip on her bag, feeling the comforting weight of the flashlight and notebook inside. It wasn't much, but it gave her a semblance of control in an otherwise chaotic situation. Garrett, on the other hand, seemed far more at ease than she expected, his shotgun slung casually over his shoulder as if he'd long since accepted the dangers around them.

"How far is the library?" Elena asked, her voice low as they passed the town square, where the statue of the town's founder loomed like a sentinel in the mist.

Luke didn't answer immediately, his focus on something ahead. "Just a few more blocks. But we have to be careful. The Order's headquarters isn't far from here."

At the mention of the Order, Elena's nerves spiked. She glanced around, half-expecting hooded figures to emerge from the shadows. The idea of them controlling the town from behind the scenes felt surreal, but the weight of the truth—especially after their encounter in the graveyard—was inescapable.

After a few more tense minutes, they arrived at the library. It was a large, imposing building, its gothic architecture worn down by years of neglect. Vines snaked up the stone walls, and the windows were fogged over, giving it an eerie, abandoned feel.

Elena hesitated at the entrance, staring up at the towering structure. "Are you sure we'll find anything here? If the Order's been around for centuries, wouldn't they have already destroyed any evidence of their existence?"

Luke's jaw tightened as he pushed open the heavy wooden door. "They've covered up a lot, but my father was convinced there were records hidden deep in the library's archives. He believed they didn't destroy everything because some members of the Order still revere the town's history."

As they stepped inside, the stale air hit Elena like a wave, thick with dust and decay. The interior was even darker than she'd expected, the tall shelves casting long shadows across the floor. Most of the books looked untouched for years, their spines cracked and fading.

Garrett whistled under his breath, surveying the dimly lit space. "Creepy as hell. You're sure there's something here?"

Luke nodded, his eyes scanning the rows of bookshelves. "There's a basement beneath the library. That's where we'll find the oldest records."

Elena shivered, her footsteps echoing in the vast, empty space as they followed Luke deeper into the library. She couldn't shake the feeling that they weren't alone—that something was watching them from the dark corners, hidden among the dust-covered books.

As they neared the back of the library, Luke led them to a narrow staircase that spiraled down into the basement. The air grew colder as they descended, and Elena's heart pounded in her chest. She didn't know what they would find down here, but every instinct screamed at her to turn back.

The basement was dimly lit by a few flickering bulbs, and the space was cluttered with old boxes, piles of newspapers, and forgotten relics. The musty smell was overpowering, and Elena covered her nose as they stepped into the narrow aisle between towering shelves.

Luke moved with purpose, his flashlight cutting through the gloom as he led them to the far corner of the basement. "This is where my father spent most of his time," he said quietly, gesturing to a small desk covered in stacks of papers and old, yellowing books. "He believed the Order's origins were buried somewhere in these archives."

Elena stepped closer, her eyes scanning the chaotic piles of documents. Most of it looked like old town records, but there was something unsettling about the way they had been left here, as if someone had been in the middle of a desperate search and never finished.

"What exactly are we looking for?" Garrett asked, glancing around nervously. "I'm not much of a reader, Grayson."

"Anything that mentions the mist," Luke replied. "Or the Order. My father believed they started as a religious sect, but something changed. They began worshipping something... older."

Elena's stomach turned at the mention of worship. The thought of people venerating an ancient force that fed on fear and souls was almost too much to comprehend. But as she began sifting through the papers, her hands shaking slightly, she knew she couldn't stop now. They were too close.

After what felt like hours of searching, Elena pulled out a fragile, leather-bound journal from the bottom of a stack. The cover was worn, and the pages inside were brittle, but as she flipped through them, her breath caught in her throat.

"Luke," she whispered, holding up the journal. "I think I found something."

He hurried over, his flashlight illuminating the faded handwriting. As he read the entries, his expression darkened.

"What is it?" Garrett asked, stepping closer.

Luke's voice was tight with tension as he read aloud. "It's a journal from one of the original founders of the town. He talks about discovering the mist in the forest—the same mist we saw. But he describes it as a 'gift'—something that would protect the town and give them power."

Elena's heart sank. "So they *wanted* it?"

Luke nodded grimly. "At first, yes. But the entries change. He talks about how the mist became uncontrollable, how it started taking people. That's when they formed the Order—to contain it, to control its hunger. They made sacrifices to keep it at bay."

The words hung heavy in the air. Sacrifices. Elena felt a sickening twist in her gut. The Order wasn't just trying to control the town—they were feeding the mist, keeping it alive through blood and fear.

"They've been doing this for centuries," Luke continued, his voice thick with anger. "Taking people, feeding the mist, keeping the town under their control."

Garrett let out a low whistle. "So, what's their endgame? Why keep the town in this state?"

Elena flipped to the last page of the journal, her eyes narrowing as she read the final entry. "It says here that the mist is tied to something deep beneath the town. The founder called it 'the Shadow's heart.' It's not just the mist—it's something else, something that the Order is protecting."

Luke clenched his fists. "We need to find it. If we destroy the heart, maybe we can stop the mist."

Garrett raised an eyebrow. "And how exactly do we do that? Just waltz into the Order's lair and blow it up?"

Elena glanced at Luke, her mind racing. They didn't have all the answers yet, but they were closer than they'd ever been. If they could find this "heart," they might stand a chance at stopping the Order and freeing Hollow's End from its nightmare.

But the deeper they dug, the more dangerous it became. The Order would know they were getting close. And the mist wasn't the only thing that was hunting them.

"We need to move fast," Luke said, tucking the journal into his bag. "If the Order finds out we've been here..."

A sudden sound cut him off—a soft rustling, like the shifting of fabric in the darkness.

They weren't alone.

Elena's pulse quickened, and she exchanged a look with Luke. Whatever was lurking in the shadows of the library basement, it wasn't friendly.

The mist had found them.

Chapter 7. The Cloaked Threat

The rustling grew louder, the sound unmistakable in the suffocating silence of the library basement. Elena froze, her heart thudding in her chest, as her eyes darted toward the shadows at the far end of the room. A figure emerged from the darkness, draped in a black cloak that seemed to merge with the gloom. The figure's hood was pulled low, concealing its face, but the faint glow of something sinister flickered beneath the cloak, like embers in the void.

Elena instinctively backed up, bumping into Luke. His hand went to the gun at his waist, though he hesitated. The figure didn't move any closer but stood silently, watching them. Garrett, who had been scanning the room nervously, swore under his breath and gripped his shotgun.

"Elena..." Luke's voice was barely a whisper. "Don't move."

She glanced at him, fear tightening her throat. "What is that?"

The cloaked figure took a step forward, its movement unnaturally smooth, as if it glided rather than walked. In its hand, it clutched something small and metallic—a pendant of some kind, its surface etched with strange, swirling symbols.

"You've been searching where you shouldn't," the figure's voice hissed from beneath the hood. It was low and distorted, as if it came from somewhere far away, not quite human.

Elena's blood ran cold. "Who are you?"

The figure tilted its head slightly, as if amused by the question. "I am a servant of the Order. You are trespassing in sacred ground."

Luke's grip tightened on his weapon, but his voice remained steady. "We know what you're doing. We know about the sacrifices, about the mist. We're going to stop you."

A soft, unsettling laugh escaped the figure. "Stop us? You don't understand what you're dealing with. The mist is eternal. It has existed long before this town, and it will continue long after you're gone."

Elena took a step forward, her fear giving way to anger. "You're murdering innocent people. For centuries, you've been feeding them to that... thing in the mist. How can you call that protection?"

The figure was silent for a moment, as if contemplating her words. Then it raised a hand, the pendant swinging gently back and forth in its grip. "The mist requires balance. We offer sacrifices to keep it sated, to maintain control. Without us, the mist would devour everything. You think you can stop it? You will only bring about your own destruction."

Before Elena could respond, Luke stepped in front of her, his voice hard. "We're not afraid of you or the Order. Tell your masters they can't hide anymore. We're going to find the Shadow's heart and destroy it."

At the mention of the heart, the figure stiffened, its hooded face turning sharply toward Luke. "You speak of things you do not understand, boy. The heart is not for mortals to touch."

Garrett raised his shotgun. "Why don't you let us worry about that?"

The figure's posture shifted, as if it were preparing for something. In an instant, the room grew colder, the temperature plummeting so fast that Elena could see her breath mist in front of her. The shadows around the figure seemed to ripple, spreading out like tendrils across the floor.

"Enough talk," the figure hissed. "You have meddled too long in the Order's affairs. It is time for the mist to claim you."

Without warning, the figure raised its hand, and the pendant glowed with an eerie light. The mist surged into the room, thick and fast, swirling around them in a suffocating cloud. Elena gasped as the cold fog wrapped around her, blinding her, making it impossible to see Luke or Garrett.

"Luke!" she shouted, reaching out blindly. Her fingers grasped nothing but cold air. Panic gripped her chest as the mist coiled tighter, its tendrils seeming to whisper in her ears, filling her mind with distorted voices. The voices were familiar, haunting—her mother, her father, calling her name.

"Elena… Elena… come to us…"

"No!" she cried, stumbling back, fighting to keep her mind clear. The mist pressed in closer, and for a terrifying moment, she felt as if she were being pulled into the fog itself, her consciousness slipping away. The cold was unbearable, a bone-deep chill that gnawed at her senses.

But then, through the fog, she felt something warm—Luke's hand, grabbing her arm, yanking her back. His voice broke through the chaos. "Elena, stay with me! Don't listen to it!"

She latched onto his voice, grounding herself in the present. The mist still swirled around them, but she could see his face now, sharp and focused. Garrett appeared a moment later, his eyes wild but determined as he aimed his shotgun into the mist.

"We need to get out of here!" Garrett shouted over the howling wind. "This thing isn't gonna let us leave alive!"

Luke's eyes darted toward the cloaked figure, which stood at the far end of the room, its form almost indistinguishable from the shadows now. "We can't leave without stopping it. If we don't, the Order will keep coming after us. The mist will keep hunting."

Elena knew he was right, but the mist was relentless, pressing closer, colder, with every second. The figure seemed to grow larger, more menacing, as if feeding off their fear.

In desperation, Elena grabbed the journal from Luke's bag and flipped to the last page—the one that had mentioned the heart. "There has to be something in here," she muttered, scanning the faded writing. Her eyes landed on a single phrase, written in jagged script:

To sever the heart, the pendant must be broken.

Her gaze shot up to the pendant in the figure's hand. It was the key. The pendant wasn't just a symbol—it was tied to the heart of the mist, to the source of its power.

"Luke, the pendant!" she shouted, her voice strained. "We have to destroy it!"

Luke's eyes narrowed, and he nodded. "Garrett, cover me!"

Garrett raised his shotgun, firing a blast into the swirling mist as Luke charged forward. The cloaked figure hissed in anger, raising the pendant high above its head. The mist surged in response, lashing out like a living thing. But Luke was fast, ducking under the tendrils of fog as he sprinted toward the figure.

Elena's heart pounded in her chest as she watched Luke close the distance. The figure moved to strike, but Luke was already on it. With a swift, powerful motion, he grabbed the pendant from the figure's hand, tearing it free.

The moment his fingers closed around it, the mist screamed—a terrible, high-pitched wail that echoed through the basement. The cloaked figure staggered back, its form flickering, as if it were losing its grip on reality.

Luke didn't hesitate. He slammed the pendant to the ground and stomped on it with all his strength.

The pendant shattered, sending shards of light exploding into the mist. The effect was immediate. The mist recoiled, writhing in agony as the room brightened, the oppressive cold lifting. The figure let out a guttural roar as its body dissolved into the shadows, swallowed by the collapsing fog.

Elena collapsed to her knees, gasping for breath as the last of the mist dissipated, leaving the basement eerily still.

Luke knelt beside her, breathing hard but steady. "It's over," he said, his voice rough but triumphant.

Garrett lowered his shotgun, his face pale but relieved. "That... was way too close."

Elena nodded, still trying to process what had just happened. They had done it—they had destroyed the pendant, severed the heart. But even as relief washed over her, she knew deep down that this was far from the end.

The mist might be gone, for now, but the Order wasn't. And they would not take kindly to this defeat.

Chapter 8. Shadows of the Past

The silence in the library basement was deafening after the mist's departure, but it was not a peaceful silence. It felt as though the air had been sucked out of the room, leaving an empty, suffocating void. Elena, Luke, and Garrett remained still, each trying to steady their breath and make sense of what had just happened.

For a moment, there was a fragile sense of victory. The cloaked figure was gone, and the mist had retreated. But Elena's skin prickled with unease. Something didn't feel right.

Luke stood first, dusting off his hands after crushing the pendant. His eyes scanned the room, not with relief, but with cautious expectation. "This isn't over," he muttered.

Garrett raised an eyebrow, still catching his breath. "What are you talking about? We destroyed that freaky pendant thing, and the mist's gone. Isn't that the whole point?"

Elena pushed herself up, her legs still weak from the terror that had gripped her moments ago. "The pendant was just part of it," she said softly, echoing Luke's wariness. "The journal mentioned the heart... but what if the heart is more than just this pendant? What if it's something deeper?"

Luke nodded, his expression dark. "The Order's been feeding the mist for centuries. They wouldn't rely on just one pendant to protect something that powerful. There has to be more—another way they're keeping control."

Garrett let out a heavy sigh, looking around the room as though searching for a quick escape. "Great. So, we're back at square one, then? Just deeper in the rabbit hole?"

Before anyone could answer, there was a sudden sound from above—the unmistakable creak of footsteps on the floorboards. Elena's heart lurched, and Luke's hand immediately went to his gun. Garrett, gripping his shotgun tightly, motioned for them to stay quiet.

"Someone's upstairs," Luke whispered, his voice tense. "We need to move."

They quickly extinguished their flashlights and crept toward the staircase. The air felt thick with dread as they moved silently, trying to make out the sounds from above. The library's upper floors had been empty when they entered—abandoned for years, like much of Hollow's End—but now, there was no denying the presence of someone, or something, pacing slowly, deliberately, through the aisles of books above.

Elena's mind raced as they ascended the steps. Was it more members of the Order? Had they come to retrieve the pendant or finish what their cloaked servant had started? And if so, how many were there?

Luke led the way, his eyes focused and sharp. He gestured for them to fan out as they reached the top of the stairs, scanning the darkened shelves. The flicker of lantern light caught Elena's eye, and her pulse quickened as she saw two figures near the entrance of the library.

They were talking in hushed tones, their backs turned to Elena and the others. Both wore long, dark coats—too formal for ordinary townspeople, and far too clean for those who lived in Hollow's End. One of them, a man with slicked-back hair, held a lantern, casting eerie shadows across the walls. The other, a woman with sharp, angular features, had her arms folded across her chest, looking impatient.

"We need to move faster," the woman snapped. "The pendant is missing. They've already been here."

The man looked agitated, his fingers drumming on the lantern's handle. "I know, but the heart is still protected. Without the pendant, they won't get far."

Elena's breath caught in her throat. They *were* from the Order. She pressed herself closer to the bookshelf, trying to stay hidden as she strained to hear more.

The woman stepped forward, her voice lowering to a conspiratorial tone. "We need to inform the council. They won't be pleased that the pendant has been destroyed. It means they're getting closer to uncovering the heart."

The man sighed, his shoulders slumping slightly. "The council will have our heads if we fail. Do you think they'll really let us walk out of this if they find out the pendant's gone?"

Before the woman could respond, Garrett's foot slipped on a loose floorboard behind them, the sharp creak breaking the tense silence. Both members of the Order spun around, their eyes narrowing in alarm.

"Who's there?" the woman barked, reaching into her coat for something—probably a weapon.

Elena felt her heart leap into her throat, but Luke acted fast. He surged forward, grabbing the man and slamming him into the nearest bookshelf, disarming him with practiced ease. The woman barely had time to react before Garrett leveled his shotgun at her chest.

"Don't move," Garrett warned, his voice deadly calm.

The woman's eyes darted between them, calculating. But instead of panicking, she simply raised her hands, a cold smile curling her lips. "You don't know what you're doing. This isn't going to end well for any of you."

Elena stepped forward, her pulse still racing. "What do you mean by the heart? What are you protecting?"

The woman's smile widened, her eyes gleaming with dark amusement. "You're in way over your heads. The heart is not something you can simply destroy. It's ancient, older than this town, older than anything you can imagine."

Luke tightened his grip on the man he held against the shelf. "Where is it?"

The woman's smile faltered slightly, but her defiance remained. "You think you can just waltz into the heart of the mist and destroy it? The Order has guarded it for generations. If you keep pushing, you'll meet the same fate as those before you."

Garrett glanced at Luke, then back at the woman. "We've handled worse than this."

Elena could feel the tension rising in the air, thick and electric. She knew they were on the verge of something big, but there was still so much they didn't understand. The heart—whatever it was—wasn't just an object. It was something more powerful, more dangerous than they had anticipated.

Before she could ask another question, the man in Luke's grip let out a low, eerie laugh. "You really don't get it, do you? The heart is the town. It's Hollow's End. You can't destroy it without destroying everything."

His words sent a chill down Elena's spine. Hollow's End *was* the heart? It didn't make sense, but the way he said it, with such certainty, made her blood run cold.

Luke shoved him harder into the shelf. "Start explaining. What is the heart, and how do we stop it?"

The man winced but maintained his grin. "You can't stop it. It's not just a thing—it's alive. The mist, the heart, the Order… we are all connected. If you destroy the heart, you destroy Hollow's End. You destroy everything."

A tense silence followed his words, and Elena's mind raced to process what he had just revealed. Could it be true? Was the heart so deeply entwined with the town that destroying it would mean obliterating everything and everyone in Hollow's End?

The woman's cold voice interrupted her thoughts. "You think you're heroes, but you don't understand the cost of what you're trying to do."

Luke's jaw clenched. "I'd rather destroy everything than let this nightmare continue."

Before anyone could react, the woman made her move. In a lightning-fast motion, she pulled a blade from her coat and slashed at Garrett's shotgun, knocking it out of his hands. At the same moment, the man twisted in Luke's grip and broke free, shoving him back.

Chaos erupted. Elena stumbled back as the woman lunged toward her, the glinting blade aimed straight at her heart.

Chapter 9. Descent into Darkness

Elena barely had time to react as the woman lunged at her, the blade slicing through the air with deadly precision. Instinct kicked in, and she twisted to the side just in time, the knife grazing her arm instead of plunging into her chest. Pain seared through her skin, but she pushed it aside, adrenaline fueling her next move. She grabbed a nearby chair and swung it, knocking the woman off balance.

Luke, regaining his footing, charged at the man who had broken free from his grip. The man was faster than he looked, but Luke tackled him, the two crashing into a nearby bookshelf. Books tumbled to the floor as the fight intensified, each of them grappling for control.

Garrett, still stunned from having his shotgun knocked away, scrambled to retrieve it, but the woman was quick. She kicked the gun across the floor, sending it skittering out of reach before spinning toward Elena again, her eyes alight with fury.

"You don't know what you're meddling with, girl," the woman hissed, circling Elena like a predator. "You think you're saving this town? You're condemning it."

Elena's mind raced as she tried to stay calm. The pain in her arm throbbed, but she couldn't let it distract her. She needed to think. The woman was faster, stronger—likely trained by the Order. If Elena wanted to survive, she had to outsmart her.

"You're killing innocent people," Elena said, trying to stall as she glanced around for something—anything—she could use as a weapon. "Sacrificing them to the mist. How is that saving anyone?"

The woman smirked, her grip tightening on the blade. "The mist keeps the balance. Without it, the heart would consume everything. The Order makes the necessary sacrifices so that the town can survive. You think you can stop us? You don't understand what's at stake."

Elena's gaze flicked to a heavy bookend on a nearby table. She just needed to get close enough. "Maybe you're the ones who don't understand," Elena shot back, edging toward the bookend. "What kind of life is it, living under the constant threat of the mist? People are living in fear, in pain. There has to be a better way."

The woman's expression hardened, and she stepped forward, her blade raised for another strike. "There is no other way."

In that split second, Elena lunged for the bookend. She grabbed it and swung it with all her might, catching the woman off guard. The heavy metal struck her arm, and the knife clattered to the ground. The woman let out a hiss of pain, clutching her arm as she staggered back.

Luke, meanwhile, had managed to pin the man to the ground, his fist colliding with the man's jaw in a series of quick, brutal strikes. The man groaned, blood trickling from his nose, but he was still fighting back, his hands scrambling for something—anything—to turn the tide.

Garrett, now weaponless, charged toward the woman, tackling her to the floor before she could recover. The two of them tumbled in a blur of fists and fury, but Garrett's raw strength overpowered her, pinning her to the ground.

"Stay down," he growled, his breath ragged.

Elena rushed to help, but the woman's eyes gleamed with a dangerous glint. "You're all fools. The heart will come for you. You can't stop it. None of you can."

Elena knelt beside her, staring into those cold, calculating eyes. "Where is the heart?" she demanded. "How do we stop it?"

The woman's smirk returned, blood staining her lips. "You won't find it. You'll die before you get close."

Luke, now restraining the man with a makeshift rope of torn curtain fabric, glanced up at Elena. "She's not going to tell us anything. They're too deep into this."

The man coughed, blood speckling his chin as he sneered at Luke. "It's already too late. The heart is awakening. You've disturbed the balance, and now the town will pay the price."

A cold chill settled over the room as his words hung in the air. Elena exchanged a glance with Luke and Garrett. The air felt different, heavy with something unseen. The hairs on the back of her neck stood on end, and a deep, instinctual fear gripped her.

"What's happening?" Garrett asked, his voice low.

Elena's heart raced as she stood, her gaze darting around the dimly lit library. "We need to leave. Now."

Luke nodded, grabbing the man by the collar and hauling him to his feet. "We're taking them with us. Maybe once we're out of here, we can—"

He didn't get to finish his sentence. The ground beneath their feet trembled violently, sending books and debris crashing to the floor. The sound was deafening, like the earth itself was groaning in pain. Elena stumbled, grabbing onto a nearby shelf to steady herself.

"What the hell is that?" Garrett shouted over the noise, his eyes wide with alarm.

The man laughed, a twisted, mocking sound. "You're too late. It's waking up."

Before anyone could react, the floor beneath them began to crack, jagged lines snaking across the tiles like lightning. From the fractures, a thick, black mist started to rise, seeping into the air. It was colder than before, more aggressive, swirling faster as if it had a mind of its own.

"The mist..." Elena whispered, her stomach twisting with dread. "It's coming from below."

Luke yanked the man toward the exit. "We need to get out of here, *now*!"

But the mist was spreading too fast. It engulfed the room, blinding them, choking them with its icy tendrils. Elena gasped, trying to fight it off, but it clung to her, pulling at her limbs, her mind.

The whispers returned—faint at first, then louder, more insistent. Voices she recognized. Her mother's voice. Her father's. "Elena... come to us..."

"No!" she cried, struggling against the mist. It was trying to consume her, to pull her into whatever dark place it came from. She could feel its malevolent intent, like it was alive, hungry for her soul.

"Elena!" Luke's voice cut through the chaos, and she felt his hand grip her arm, yanking her back from the edge of the mist's pull. His face was pale, his eyes wide with fear, but his grip was strong, anchoring her to reality.

"We have to go!" he shouted, pulling her toward the exit.

Garrett was already dragging the woman, who was now unconscious from the struggle, but the man was laughing, even as the mist swirled around him. "You can't escape it," he taunted. "The heart is awake. It's calling for you."

Luke ignored him, his focus solely on getting Elena and Garrett out of the library. They stumbled through the mist, coughing and choking on the thick fog, but they managed to reach the door, bursting into the cold night air.

The mist didn't follow them outside. It stayed contained within the library, swirling like a living storm, but they could still feel its malevolent presence, watching, waiting.

Elena collapsed onto the grass, gasping for breath. Her arm throbbed, her mind reeling from the whispers that still echoed in her head. She looked back at the library, its windows now dark and foreboding.

"The heart is under the town," she whispered, realization dawning on her. "That's why the mist is so strong here. The heart is buried beneath Hollow's End."

Luke knelt beside her, his expression grim. "Then we dig. We find it, and we destroy it."

Garrett, still catching his breath, looked between them, his face pale. "How? How do we destroy something that's keeping this entire town alive?"

Elena didn't have an answer. But one thing was clear—the heart was awake, and it wasn't going to stop until it consumed everything.

Chapter 10. The Heart of Hollow's End

The cold night air bit at Elena's skin as she stared at the library, its windows now shrouded in the swirling mist, the eerie presence of the heart awakening beneath the town. Luke, Garrett, and their two captives stood beside her, equally haunted by what they had just encountered.

Everything had led them to this moment. The Order, the sacrifices, the mist, and now, the heart—buried beneath Hollow's End, pulsing with a life force they couldn't fully comprehend.

"We need to go underground," Elena said, her voice barely a whisper, as if speaking too loudly might summon the darkness they were about to face.

Luke nodded, his jaw set with determination. "There are tunnels beneath the town. Old mining shafts from when Hollow's End was first settled. The journal mentioned them."

Garrett wiped the sweat from his brow, glancing warily at their prisoners. "We're bringing them with us? Can we trust they won't try something again?"

Elena studied the man and woman from the Order, both of whom were bruised but still defiant. They had failed to stop them from discovering the truth, but that didn't mean they were powerless. Even now, the man wore a twisted smile, as if he knew something they didn't.

"We don't have a choice," Elena said. "They know more about the heart than we do. If we leave them here, the Order will find them and regroup. If we take them, we might be able to force more answers out of them."

Luke and Garrett exchanged a glance, but neither argued. Time was running out, and they all felt it—the growing pressure of something ancient and angry stirring beneath the earth.

They bound the captives' hands with strips of torn fabric, leaving just enough slack for them to walk. The woman's eyes burned with fury, but she remained silent, while the man continued to sneer, a constant reminder that they weren't in control.

Luke led the way, guiding them through the abandoned streets of Hollow's End, past crumbling buildings and deserted homes. The mist hung in the air like a predator waiting to strike, watching their every move. Every shadow seemed to twitch with life, and the whispers in the wind grew louder the closer they got to their destination.

"The entrance to the tunnels is just ahead," Luke said, his voice low.

They stopped in front of an old, boarded-up mine entrance on the outskirts of town. The wooden boards had rotted, and the ground around the opening was overgrown with weeds. It looked like it hadn't been touched in decades, but Elena felt the pull of something deeper, something ancient, calling to her from within the earth.

"This is it," Garrett muttered, gripping his shotgun tighter. "I don't like this."

"No one does," Elena replied, taking a deep breath to steady her nerves.

Luke used the butt of his gun to pry off the boards, the wood splintering with a sickening crack. Once the entrance was clear, they shined their flashlights into the darkness below. The tunnel stretched into the earth, a gaping maw that seemed to swallow the light, as if even the beams of their flashlights were afraid to venture too far.

"Stay close," Luke warned as they descended into the tunnel.

The air grew colder as they made their way deeper into the earth. The walls of the tunnel were damp, and the sound of dripping water echoed eerily around them. Elena kept glancing over her shoulder, half-expecting the mist to follow them, but for now, it remained aboveground.

They walked in tense silence, the only sound the shuffle of their feet on the dirt floor and the occasional soft grunt from their captives. The deeper they went, the stronger the feeling of unease became, as though the very ground beneath them was alive, watching, waiting for them to reach their destination.

"Do you feel that?" Garrett whispered after a while, his voice barely audible in the oppressive darkness. "Like the air is… vibrating."

Elena nodded. She felt it too—a low, thrumming sensation beneath her feet, like the pulse of a living thing. They were getting close.

Suddenly, the tunnel opened up into a wide underground chamber, and Elena's breath caught in her throat. The heart of Hollow's End.

In the center of the chamber, illuminated by the dim light of their flashlights, was a massive stone altar. Above it, suspended in the air by thick, twisting roots, was a large, pulsating mass of black mist. It writhed and pulsed like a living organism, tendrils of darkness stretching out in all directions, connecting to the roots that disappeared into the earth.

Elena felt a wave of nausea wash over her as she gazed at the heart. It was more terrifying than anything she had imagined. This was the source of the mist—the source of the evil that had plagued Hollow's End for centuries.

"The heart," Luke breathed, his voice barely a whisper. "It's alive."

Garrett stepped forward, his eyes wide with disbelief. "How do we destroy something like that?"

Before anyone could answer, the man from the Order let out a harsh laugh. "You can't," he said, his voice filled with triumph. "The heart is eternal. It's the lifeblood of Hollow's End. If you destroy it, the town will die. The people will die."

Elena's stomach twisted. Could it be true? Could the heart be so deeply connected to the town that destroying it would mean the end of everything?

"We can't just let it live," Luke growled, his hands trembling with barely contained fury. "Not after everything it's done. All the people it's killed."

The woman from the Order, her voice cold and calculating, spoke for the first time in what felt like hours. "You think you can destroy it? Even if you could, the mist would consume you before you got close enough. You're fools, all of you."

Elena's mind raced as she tried to think. There had to be a way. They couldn't let the heart continue to feed on the people of Hollow's End. But they also couldn't risk destroying the town and everyone in it.

"We need to sever the connection," she said suddenly, her voice trembling with urgency. "The roots—it's feeding off the town through the roots. If we cut them off, maybe it'll weaken the heart."

Garrett raised an eyebrow. "And how do we do that?"

Elena glanced at the thick, gnarled roots that stretched out from the heart and into the earth. "We burn them. If we can destroy enough of the roots, maybe the heart will be weakened enough for us to finish it."

Luke's expression hardened as he pulled out his lighter. "Let's do it."

Garrett and Luke moved quickly, dousing the roots with kerosene they had packed for emergencies. As soon as they lit the flames, the roots began to sizzle and crackle, black smoke rising into the air.

The heart reacted instantly. It let out a low, guttural roar that reverberated through the chamber, shaking the walls and sending a wave of cold air rushing through the tunnel. The mist surrounding it thickened, its tendrils thrashing violently as it struggled to maintain its connection to the town.

"It's working!" Elena shouted, backing away from the heart as the flames spread across the roots.

But just as the heart began to weaken, the mist surged forward, engulfing the chamber in a thick, choking fog. Elena gasped, her vision blurring as the cold tendrils of mist wrapped around her, pulling her toward the altar.

"Elena!" Luke shouted, his voice muffled by the mist.

She struggled against the pull, but the mist was too strong. It was dragging her toward the heart, toward the very thing she had come to destroy. She could feel its malevolent presence pressing down on her, whispering in her mind, calling her to give in, to let go.

But she wouldn't. She couldn't.

With one final burst of strength, she reached into her jacket and pulled out the broken pendant. The same one they had destroyed in the library. The mist recoiled at the sight of it, its grip loosening for just a moment.

"Elena, now!" Luke's voice cut through the fog.

With all her strength, she threw the pendant into the flames, watching as it was consumed by the fire. The heart let out a deafening scream, its tendrils thrashing wildly as the flames spread to the altar.

For a moment, everything went still.

And then, the heart exploded in a blinding flash of light.

Elena was thrown backward, her head spinning as the shockwave rippled through the chamber. When she finally opened her eyes, the mist was gone. The heart was gone. Only the charred remains of the roots remained, smoldering in the ashes.

She sat up, her chest heaving with exhaustion. Luke and Garrett were beside her, equally dazed but alive.

"It's over," she whispered, tears of relief filling her eyes. "It's finally over."

Hollow's End was free.

The End.

Milton Keynes UK
Ingram Content Group UK Ltd.
UKHW020047181024
449757UK00011B/564